W9-AZT-441

Febold Feboldson

ARIANE DEWEY

GREENWILLOW BOOKS · NEW YORK

FOR EDDIE KOUFLIE

28875

Copyright © 1984 by Ariane Dewey
All rights reserved. No part of this book may be reproduced or utilized in
any form or by any means, electronic or mechanical, including photocopying,
recording or by any information storage and retrieval system, without
permission in writing from the Publisher, Greenwillow Books, a division of
William Morrow & Company, Inc., 105 Madison Ave., New York, N.Y. 10016.
Printed in the United States of America   First Edition
1 2 3 4 5 6 7 8 9 10

Library of Congress Cataloging in Publication Data
Dewey, Ariane.   Febold Feboldson.
Summary: The Nebraska farmer conquers
cyclones, blizzards, fog, and
grasshoppers in incredible ways.
1. Feboldson, Febold (Legendary character) —
Juvenile literature. [1. Feboldson,
Febold (Legendary character) 2. Folklore —
United States. 3. Tall tales] I. Title.
PZ8.1.D54Fe 1984   398.2'2'0973 [E]
83-14222   ISBN 0-688-02533-1
ISBN 0-688-02534-X (lib. bdg.)

CONTENTS

THE YEAR THE SNOW
WOULDN'T MELT

Febold Feboldson was the first farmer to come to the Great Plains. He settled in what is now Nebraska.

He liked it fine, except for the weather.
There were floods, blizzards, and heat
waves, all on the same day. Cyclones
whirled dust back and forth from the
Rocky Mountains to the Mississippi River.

Other settlers came, but they didn't stay.
Febold stayed. It didn't take him long to
figure out how to deal with the weather.

One year the snow froze so hard, it didn't
even melt when summer came. The year was
1848. That was the year gold was discovered
in California. Fishermen, firemen, butchers,
carpenters, people from the city and
people from the country left their
work and headed west.
"We're miners now," they shouted.
But the Gold Rush was held up. The snow
lay in drifts forty feet high. The miners
couldn't cross the plains.
But Febold could.

He drove his wagon to Death Valley and loaded it with desert sand.

Desert sand never cools off.

He sold it to the miners. They used it to melt the snow.

And that is how the miners got to California in time to be called forty-niners.

THE YEAR
OF THE BIG RAIN

The year started out dry. And it got drier and hotter, hotter and drier. The streams dried up. Febold couldn't go fishing.
"Now that's enough!" he said.
A frog was sitting nearby. Febold splashed it with water from a bucket.
"It's raining!" Febold shouted.

The frog croaked the news to his friends. Soon all the frogs on the prairie were croaking, "Rain! Rain!" They made such a din, it sounded like thunder.

Some clouds in the north heard it.
"Thunder!" they cried, and hurried south.
They didn't want to miss the storm.

It rained so hard that the frogs were washed down to the Gulf of Mexico. It took them nine months to hop back.

THE YEAR
OF THE STRIPED WEATHER

The sun shone on Febold's cornfield. At the same time the rain fell on his cane field, which was just up the hill.

The sun was so hot that the corn popped.

It rained so hard the sugar washed out
of the cane stalks.

The syrup ran down into the cornfield.
It swept the popcorn into balls. They
were huge.
"Those look good enough to eat," said
Febold.
And he ate them all winter long.

THE YEAR
OF THE CYCLONES

At last someone settled near Febold.
His name was Eldad Johnson.
"Does the wind always blow like this?"
he asked.
"No," Febold replied. "Sometimes it
blows harder."

One calm afternoon, Eldad Johnson's grandfather climbed up their windmill to oil the gears. Just then a cyclone whirled by. It blew the old man off the windmill.

It dropped him flat on his back. All the
breath was knocked out of him.
Eldad and Febold thought he was dead.
Febold built a coffin for him. They dug
his grave near the Dismal River.

Suddenly another cyclone spun up. It blew
the coffin away. Eldad's grandfather fell out.
The storm blew the breath right back into
him. It dropped him on his windmill.

When Eldad got home, there was his grandfather. "Wind sure is fierce today," the old man said.

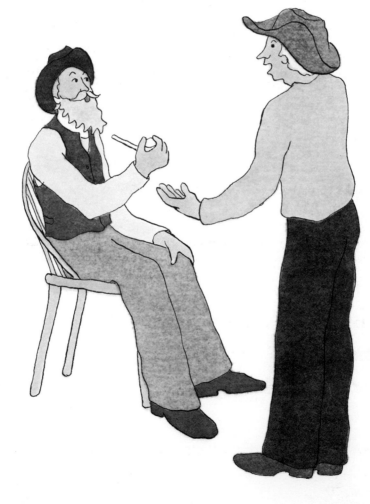

THE YEAR
OF THE GREAT HEAT

It was so hot, iron pots melted. All kinds
of animals crawled into Febold's house.
It was the only shade around.
Soon Febold had a lot of pets.

Peggy was a three-legged cat. Febold made a
wooden leg for her. She used it to club rats.

Lizzie was Febold's pet gopher. She dug tunnels under the house. Febold plugged them up, to trap the heat inside. He wanted to save some in case winter ever came back.

Then there was a rattlesnake named Arabella. She rattled her tail at six o'clock every morning. She made such a racket, it always woke Febold up. That made him so mad, he jumped right out of bed. Arabella was a very reliable alarm clock.

THE YEAR
OF THE FOG

One day the sky began to hiss. It
hissed louder and louder.
"What's that?" asked Eldad Johnson.
"Fog's coming," said Febold. "I'd better
order some fog-cutters."
"I don't see any fog," complained Eldad.
"You don't now, but you will soon,"
Febold said.
The air was so hot, the rain turned to
steam ten miles up. That's what caused
the hissing.

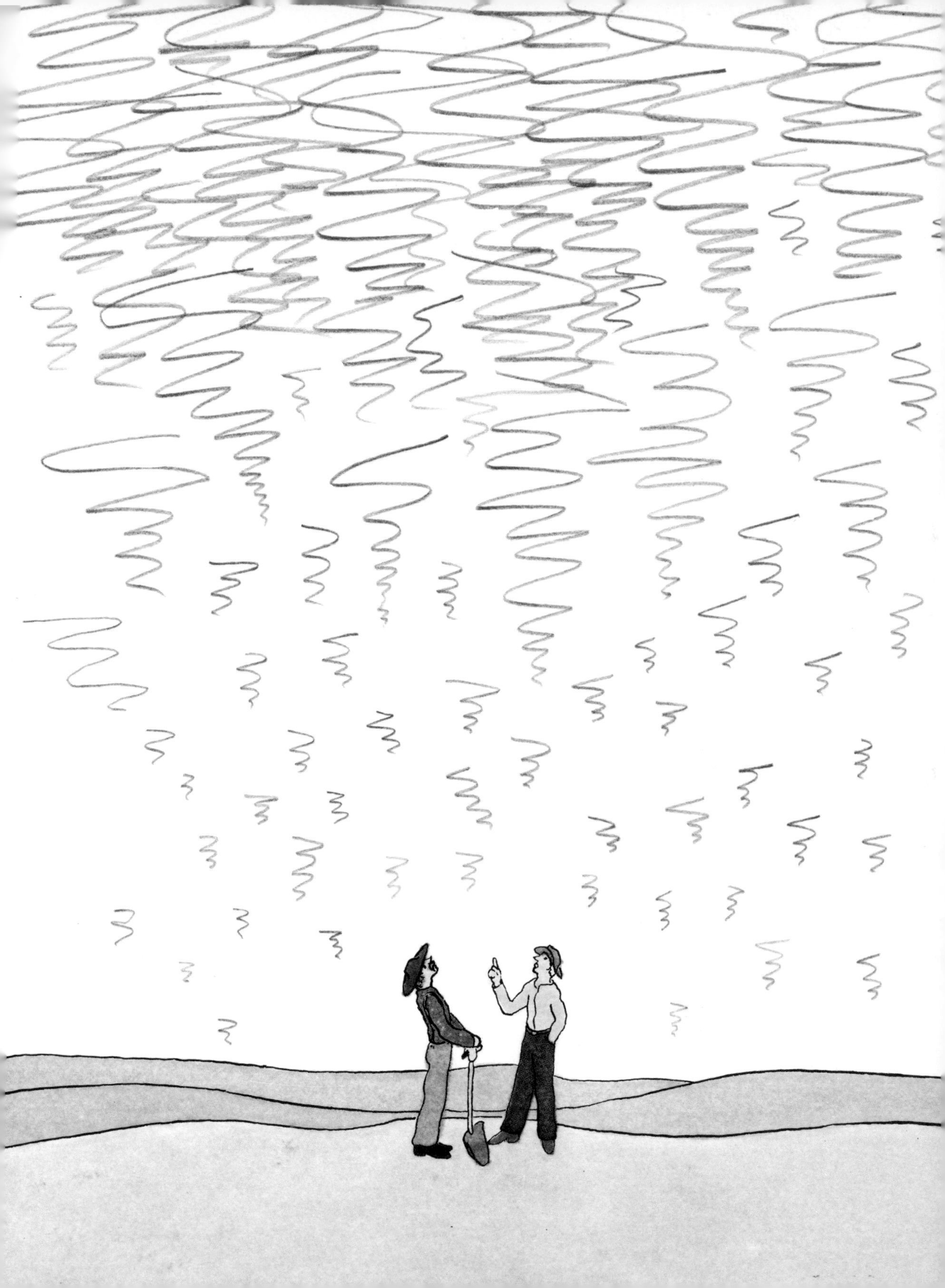

When the steam cooled, it turned into fog. The fog settled on everything. It was so thick Febold had to hold the fog open so Eldad could step through.

Ranchers didn't have to water their herds. The cattle just drank the fog. Pigs rooted around in it. Plants grew down to the sunlight on the other side of the earth.

Febold's fog-cutters finally arrived. He cut the fog into strips. He laid the strips out across the country. The strips were soon covered with dust. That's how Febold invented roads.

Now and then the fog still seeps through. That's what makes the roads so muddy.

THE YEAR
OF THE GRASSHOPPERS

Every few years grasshoppers swarmed across the plains. One year the grass hoppers ate everything in sight. They ate the crops. They ate the buffalo grass. They ate Febold's popcorn balls. There was nothing left.

Febold wrote to his aunt in New England.
He ordered a hundred hungry turkeys.
But when he let the turkeys loose, the
grasshoppers attacked them.

The hoppers chewed turkey feathers till the turkeys were bare. The birds were so upset, they ran all the way back to Massachusetts.

The grasshoppers were thicker than ever. Febold swept them into sacks. They ate right through them.

Febold was furious. He grabbed a handful
of hoppers and tried to drown them in the
Dismal River. The fish gobbled them up.

"By Golly!" said Febold. "Why didn't I think of fish before?"
He imported enough flying fish to fill a prairie schooner. They swooped and soared over the plains.

"Watch 'em catch those pests!" Febold
shouted to Eldad.
When there were no grasshoppers left,
the fish flew back to the sea.

"What a place," Febold said to Eldad. "We're blown about by cyclones. We're frozen by blizzards. We're choked by dust. We're blinded by fog.

"There's no rain and the crops die. Or there's too much rain and the floods wash the crops away. If the floods don't get them, the grasshoppers do.

FEBOLD FEBOLDSON   3
DEWEY ARIANE   J398.2DEW   22098

          J   28875
        398.2
        Dew

        Dewey, Ariane

          Febold Feboldson